I Want to Help!

For my cousins Joey, Maggie, John, Marcus, Katherine,
Annabelle, and Samantha, and for my Aunt Nini
—D. A.

To Tom
—N. H.

Published by
PEACHTREE PUBLISHERS
1700 Chattahoochee Avenue
Atlanta, Georgia 30318-2112
www.peachtree-online.com

Book design by Nancy Hayashi
Cover design by Loraine Joyner
Composition by Melanie McMahon Ives

Illustrations created in watercolor, pen, and colored pencil. Text typeset in Baskerville Infant; title typeset in Apple's Chalkduster.

Printed in April 2012 by Tien Wah in Singapore
10 9 8 7 6 5 4 3 2 1

Library of Congress Cataloging-in-Publication Data

Adams, Diane.
  I want to help! / written by Diane Adams ; illustrated by Nancy Hayashi.
    p. cm.
  Summary: Emily Pearl is good at very many things, and is the first with an offer to help her teacher, but when the school day ends and her father is late picking her up, she finds she needs a little help, too.
  ISBN 978-1-56145-630-7 / 1-56145-630-6
  [1. Stories in rhyme. 2. Schools—Fiction. 3. Helpfulness—Fiction. 4. Self-reliance—Fiction.] I. Hayashi, Nancy, ill. II. Title.
  PZ8.3.A213Te 2012
  [E]--dc23
                          2011020994

I Want to Help!

Diane Adams

illustrated by

Nancy Hayashi

PEACHTREE
ATLANTA

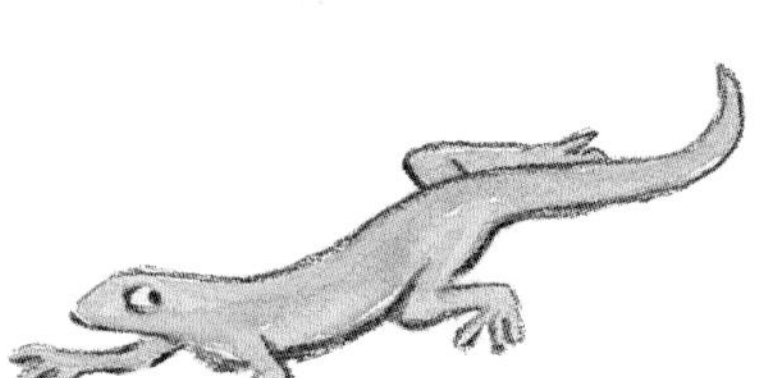

Emily Pearl is a very smart girl.

She can count to fourteen.

She can write her own name.

She can tell what is different
and what is the same.

She can do the Hokey Pokey
and jump in the air.

She can hop to the carpet
and find her own square.

And whenever Ms. Glenn
sighs, "Oh, my," to herself,
Emily Pearl says,
"I want to help!"

Emily Pearl is a very strong girl.

She can wallop the baseball and score a home run.

She can leap high in dodgeball and be the best one.

She can race all the boys and be first past the line.

She can swing on the monkey bars two at a time.

And whenever Ms. Glenn sighs, "Oh, my," to herself, Emily Pearl says, "I want to help!"

Emily Pearl is a very big girl.
She can wash her own paint can
and put it away.

She can pass out the snacks on Ms. Glenn's silver tray.

She can clean up the blocks that have crashed to the ground.

She can stack all the books that are scattered around.

And whenever Ms. Glenn
sighs, "Oh, my," to herself,
Emily Pearl says,
"I want to help!"

Emily Pearl is a very brave girl.
She can give the tarantula water and bugs.

She can let out the rabbit and clean up the rug.

She can shoo away critters
that come to the door.

And capture the crickets that hop on the floor.

But at 1:55 when
her dad isn't there,
Emily feels just a
little bit scared.

Then Ms. Glenn says, "I need you. I've so much to do.
Can you lend me a hand for a minute or two?"

And when Emily's dad finally comes down the hall,
Emily Pearl isn't frightened at all.

"Sorry I left you here all by yourself."

"Don't worry, Dad. Ms. Glenn needed my help."

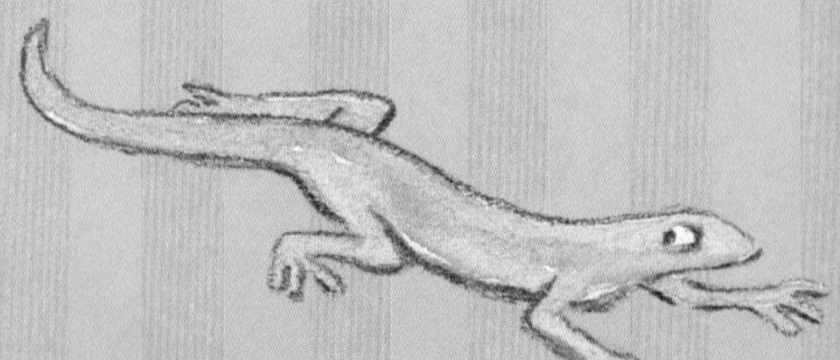